nöffy 5/08

The Muffin Fiend

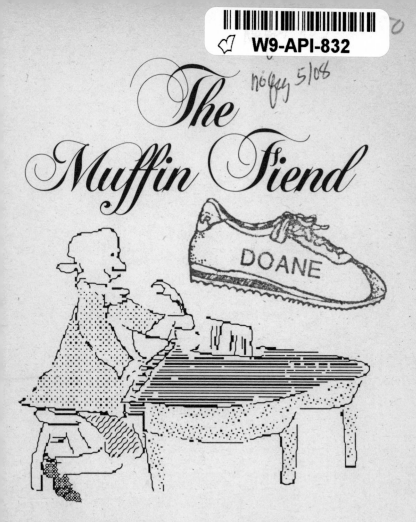

DOANE

BY DANIEL PINKWATER

A BANTAM SKYLARK BOOK®
TORONTO • NEW YORK • LONDON • SYDNEY • AUCKLAND

RL 3, 007–011

THE MUFFIN FIEND

*A Bantam Book / published by arrangement with
Lothrop, Lee & Shepard Books*

PRINTING HISTORY

Lothrop, Lee & Shepard edition published April 1986

*Skylark Books is a registered trademark of
Bantam Books, Inc. Registered in U.S. Patent and
Trademark Office and elsewhere.*

Bantam edition / November 1987

ISBN 0-553-15544-X

*Published simultaneously in the United States
and Canada*

---

*Bantam Books are published by Bantam Books, Inc. Its
trademark, consisting of the words "Bantam Books" and
the portrayal of a rooster, is Registered in U.S. Patent
and Trademark Office and in other countries. Marca
Registrada. Bantam Books, Inc., 666 Fifth Avenue,
New York, New York 10103.*

PRINTED IN THE UNITED STATES OF AMERICA

CW   0 9 8 7 6 5 4 3 2 1

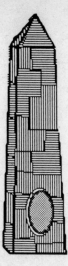

Wolfgang Amadeus Mozart, the great composer, was sitting in his office one morning, when a stranger appeared at his door.

"Herr Mozart, I want you to help me solve a mystery," the stranger said.

"Excellent!" said Mozart. "After composing great works of music, solving mysteries is my favorite activity."

"As you know," the stranger said, "Vienna is famous for pastries of all kinds."

"That is why I live in Vienna," said Mozart.

"You will be interested to know that there is a muffin fiend loose in the city," said the stranger.

"A muffin fiend?" asked Mozart.

"Exactly," said the stranger. "You do know what a muffin fiend is?"

"I used to know, but I forgot," Mozart said. "Tell me again."

"The muffin fiend is the most dangerous sort of criminal," said the stranger. "Muffin fiends can barely resist pastry in any form—but most especially, they are mad for muffins!"

"This is most interesting," said Mozart. "Tell me, who are you, and how is it that you know so much about these matters?"

"I am Inspector Charles LeChat of the French Police. I have followed the muffin fiend all the way from Paris."

"And why is this muffin fiend so dangerous?"

"I will explain that—but first, may I suggest that we take some refreshment?"

"Of course," said Mozart. "I usually have something about this time of morning myself."

Mozart called to his wife. "Constanze! Please bring us some coffee and peach muffins."

"You may have coffee," said Frau Mozart, "but there are no peach muffins."

"No peach? In that case, we will have cherry muffins," said the composer.

"There are no cherry muffins," replied Frau Mozart. "Also no cheese muffins, no raisin muffins, no gooseberry muffins, no custard muffins, no chocolate seven-layer muffins—in fact there is not a single muffin of any description to be had in all of Vienna."

"Now I see why you are so anxious to stop this monster!" Mozart said.

"Indeed," said Inspector LeChat, "as we speak my beloved city of Paris is utterly muffinless."

"It is tragic," said Mozart, "and now it appears that Vienna has suffered the same fate."

"Herr Mozart, you are the greatest genius in Europe. Please say that you will help me stop this terrible muffin fiend."

"I am now engaged in writing an opera, *The Magic Prune*. Even so, I will put aside this important work and help you stop this awful criminal," said Mozart. "Have you tried all the usual things?"

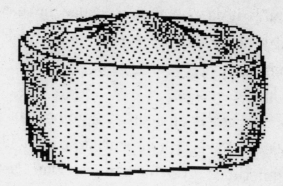

"Yes. We have no record of any professional criminal with a taste for muffins—at least on this scale. All the places where a vast number of muffins might be hidden have been searched. All the roads have been watched, and spies in foreign ports have not been able to discover any large shipments, so we believe the fiend is not smuggling the muffins."

"Then he's eating them all?" asked Mozart.

"So I believe," said LeChat.

"Remarkable. And why do you think it is only one man?"

"I think it is one man because he has been seen by several witnesses," said the French policeman.

"He has been seen?"

"Yes. He has been seen at a number of muffin bakeries in Paris. He appears to be a nobleman, and sometimes gives his name as Don Pastrami. He orders huge quantities of muffins, and then ties the baker hand and foot, and usually locks him in a closet."

"Fascinating," said the great composer. "Let us employ logic here. A city the size of Vienna must produce many thousands of muffins each day. The greatest number of muffins ever consumed by a human within twenty-four hours is one thousand and three. I know this because it is my honor to have set that record."

"Even in Paris we have heard of your accomplishment."

"Since a great many more muffins than one thousand and three are disappearing, and since we have, for the moment, no choice but to assume that the so-called Don Pastrami is eating them all—it follows that Don Pastrami is not human," Mozart explained.

"He appeared to be human," said Inspector LeChat.

"So do a lot of people," said Mozart. "Come! There's no time to lose!"

"Where are we going?" asked the policeman.

"Why, to the great Municipal Muffin Bakery!" said the great composer.

The Municipal Muffin Bakery provided ovens for the poorer citizens of Vienna. Here those who could not afford to buy muffins could bake their own for a small fee.

When Mozart and Inspector LeChat arrived, a near-riot was in progress. An angry mob was arguing with the city official in charge of the ovens.

16

"Was ist los?" asked Mozart in the local dialect.

"Ah, Herr Mozart!" said the official. "The people are angry because they came this morning with their tins of muffin mix to be baked—and when the ovens were opened just now the muffins were gone!"

"We are too late!" shouted Inspector LeChat.

"Perhaps not," said Mozart. "Has anything else unusual happened?" he asked the official.

"Only this," the official replied, "there was a nobleman here earlier—one Don Pastrami. I thought it strange that a person of wealth, as he appeared to be, should come to bake his own muffins."

"Where is this Don Pastrami now?" asked Mozart.

"I cannot say," said the official. "He disappeared during the confusion."

Mozart, meanwhile, had been looking into the window of one of the many bakeshops that lined the streets of Vienna. It was utterly empty. Not a single Viennese muffin was to be seen. It was a depressing sight. All that remained were the price cards. *Apple muffins 2 pfennigs. Blueberry muffins 3 pfennigs. Walnut muffins 4 pfennigs. Gorgonzola muffins 1 pfennig.*

"To the Wienerwald, without delay!" shouted the great genius.

"To the Vienna Woods? Why?" asked the puzzled LeChat.

"Because that is where I expect to find the elusive Don Pastrami."

"But why the woods, and not the cellars of the town, or the waterfront, or some other place?"

"The muffin fiend will be in the woods because it is remote and isolated there. That is where we will find him—and some other surprising things as well. Inspector LeChat, summon a carriage!"

In the carriage Mozart unfolded to Inspector LeChat his amazing theory that the muffin fiend, sometimes known as Don Pastrami, was in fact not of this world. LeChat found the idea hard to grasp.

"Not of this world? You mean he's dead? A ghost? A spirit?"

"No," said Mozart.

"Ah, I see," said the Frenchman. "By not of this world you mean not of the old world, comprised of Europe, Asia, and Africa. You mean to suggest that the muffin fiend is from the new world, meaning North or South America."

"No, no—that's not it," said Mozart. "By saying that the muffin fiend is not of this world, I do not mean that he is not of the world of the living, nor do I mean that he is from any unfamiliar part of this planet. I mean that he is an extraterrestrial."

"Extraterrestrial? Does that mean that he has extra toes?"

"It means that he comes not from Earth."

"Not from Earth?"

"Not."

"From not Earth?"

"I assure you."

"Then from where?"

"From another planet."

"There are other planets?"

"Oh, be quiet, you poorly informed French policeman!" said Mozart impatiently. "We've arrived in the Wienerwald."

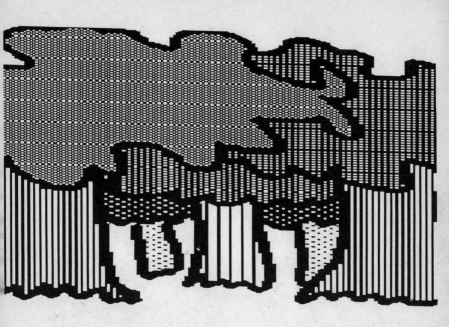

There was nothing out of the ordinary to be seen in the woods. The usual birds and animals were in evidence, and trees of course, and the odd peasant—but no muffin fiend.

"We have to trap him," said Mozart, who then removed a tiny violin from the pocket of his coat.

"Oh, do you know the muffin fiend?" Inspector LeChat asked the odd peasant.

"I never heard of him," the peasant replied.

"Well? Where is Don Pastrami?" Inspector LeChat asked Mozart.

"I used to play this when I was a very small boy," Mozart said. Then producing a tiny bow, Mozart began to play.

"What is this music?" asked LeChat.

"It is the music of the spheres," said Mozart. "It is cosmic music."

"It doesn't sound funny to me," said LeChat.

"Cosmic, not comic!" Mozart shouted. "This music will bring the extraterrestrial to us."

Mozart tuned up.
No one turned up.
Mozart fiddled.
Nothing happened.
LeChat listened.
No one appeared.

"I don't think he's coming."

"He's coming," said Mozart, strumming.

"I think he's going."

"He's not going," said Mozart, bowing.

Then a being was seen, hiding behind one tree and then another, coming closer and closer to the tuneful Wolfgang.

Then, when the flitful figure was behind the nearest tree, Mozart put down his tiny violin and baritoned, "Don Pastrami! I've come to get you!"

"You'll never get me!" sang Don Pastrami.

"You are the awful muffin fiend!"

Don Pastrami sang, "I am!"

Mozart: "Why did you take the muffins?"

Don Pastrami: "I did it. I felt like it. That's all."

Mozart: "You must have had a reason."

Don Pastrami: "I didn't have a reason. Go away."

Mozart: "Tell me. Tell me why you took the muffins."

Don Pastrami: "No!"

Mozart: "Tell me!"

Don Pastrami: "No!"

Mozart: "Tell!"

Don Pastrami: "No!"

Mozart: "Tell!"

Don Pastrami: "No!"

Mozart: "Tell! Tell!"

Don Pastrami: "No! *No!*"

Mozart: "At least shake hands to show that you're not chicken."

Don Pastrami: "O.K." (Don Pastrami shakes hands with Mozart.) "Hey! What is this? I cannot get loose!"

Mozart: "It's Viennese jiujitsu—now will you confess?"

Don Pastrami: "What choice do I have?

In the powerful grip of Mozart (who had mighty fingers from practicing the piano every day) the miserable Don Pastrami confessed: "I come from a far distant planet in a solar system you never heard of," the apprehended Pastrami said.

"As I suspected!" said the excited genius. "But there is something else—something about your voice. I've heard that voice before."

"For a time I was an opera singer. I used the name Apollo Grosso-Fortissimo."

34

"Apollo Grosso-Fortissimo! The greatest operatic tenor ever to live, up to and including most of the eighteenth century!" Mozart exclaimed. "You are my fave! Why did you quit singing?"

"The singing was only a way to earn money to buy muffins. But soon I needed many more muffins, and had to resort to stealing them."

"Such a muffin monkey! How can you eat so many?"

"I do not eat them Signor Mozart."

"Not?"

"Not."

"Not eat?"

"Not one even."

"So, what do with um?"

"Keep um."

"Keep um all?"

"Every one of um."

"For why do you keep um?"

"Keep um for fuel."

"For fuel?"

"Fuel."

"Fuel for keep warm?"

"No. Fuel for go home."

"Go home?"

"Go home. Don Pastrami go home!"

"Amazing," said Mozart.

"You said it, buster," said Don Pastrami.

"What do you think of all this?" Mozart asked
Charles LeChat.

"By the bells of Notre Dame! It amazes!" said the Frenchman.

The extraterrestrial Don Pastrami led the composer and the policeman through the forest. In a clearing they found an enormous machine. "My spaceship," said Don Pastrami.

"I don't understand," said LeChat.

"This is your ship?" asked Mozart.

"Yes."

"And the muffins?"

"Are inside." Don Pastrami led Mozart to the side of the ship and opened a little door.

"Ach, du Lieber!" Mozart exclaimed. "This thing is practically full of muffins!"

"They will power the spacecraft for my journey home," said Don Pastrami. "Rocket fuel on my planet is in solid form and very similar to the muffins of Earth."

"Do you have enough of these muffins to reach your planet?" Mozart asked.

"With the muffins I have stolen today, I have enough," said the former Apollo Grosso-Fortissimo.

"Then go," said Mozart.

"Wait!" shouted LeChat. "He is a criminal."

"If he remains on Earth, he will only steal more muffins," said Mozart. "Let's give him a pass."

"I don't know. This goes against the code of a French policeman," said Inspector LeChat.

"Be a sport," Mozart said, "and I'll dedicate a concerto to you."

"Well—seeing that it's you who's asking," Charles LeChat said.

"I'm going," said the visitor from space. "Nice planet. I had a good time."

"Drive carefully," said Mozart.

Don Pastrami climbed into his spacecraft, which took off impressively.

"This has been my strangest case," said Inspector Charles LeChat. "Now let's go get some Viennese cooking."

"I'd like to, but I have to go home and work on the Requiem," Mozart said.

"Do that later," said the French policeman. "For now come to a restaurant with me."

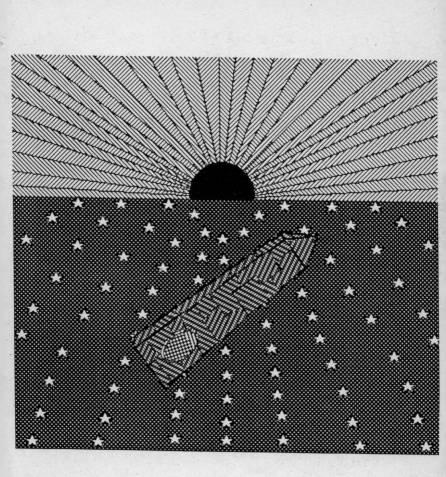

"Well, all right," said Mozart. "I am feeling hungry after solving this mystery."

"Good man," said LeChat. "Incidentally, how did you know that the man we sought was an extraterrestrial?"

"Remember when we were back at the Municipal Muffin Bakery?"

"Yes."

"Remember when I looked in the bakeshop window?"

"Certainly."

"And there were only price cards—and all the muffins were gone?"

"Yes, yes?"

"And even the Gorgonzola muffins were gone?"

"Yes, I do remember that."

"That is when I knew the man we were after was not an inhabitant of this world."

"How did you know that?" the detective asked the great genius.

"I knew that because no one on Earth would eat a Gorgonzola muffin."

End